PRAISE FOR THE FANGSTER SERIES

Readers Love the Fangster Series
Here is a sample of their comments:

About the Series

“**...**This series is a combination of two of my favorite genres: mystery and paranormal. Very fun series and I fully recommend it...” (Silversaviil on Bookbub)

“I am absolutely loving this series! It has everything I love in a good paranormal cozy mystery: 🧛 Delinquent Vampires 🐺 Protective Werewolf 🔮 Powerful Witch 🐇 Adorable Familiar 🔍 Sleuthing Fangs for the Bite was a spooktacular read and I can’t wait to see what happens next!” (Magnoliapigeon on BookBub)

Book I – Fangsters, the Novel

“A fun, original read! Vampires and witches never play well together, and when you have a hot vampire blackmailing a snarky witch into opening a school for delinquent vampires, then you know you're in for a hilarious ride that's surely not going to end well... or does it?" (Anitafuhrmann on BookBub)

"I totally loved this book. The pace was fast, the characters were certifiable, and I loved every minute of it. I am so glad I chose this book to read and the fact that it is the beginning of a series please me to no end. I can't wait for more. Fantastic book!" (Exerhombre on BookBub)

"I loved this book! The characters are interesting, with charm, sass, humour and snark. The storyline moved along at a consistent pace, and the secrets and surprises kept you guessing. The author has created an intriguing world with great characters and a well thought out lore. Definitely want to read the others in this series!" (cprokic on BookBub)

Book II – Fangs for the Bite

"A fang-tastic urban fantasy! I love the sexy dynamic between Onyx and Rebel. And now with Leroy the werewolf in the mix, it promises even more magic and mysterious hijinks. This school for naughty vampires gets better and better!" (Marianne on BookBub)

"This is supernatural/paranormal cozy at its best! A wonderful cast of quirky, funny characters who are thrown into a slightly wacky situation and are all doing their best to make it through. In this second book Rebel is dealing with the murder of a new teacher and friend. She is also caught between the world she knows and understands and the world of vampires as she tries to teach her students while solving this murder. There's lingering tension between her and Onyx head of school security and there's a few new contenders in the love life department. I'm interested to see how Revel deals with this. There's lots to love action, paranormal creatures, overly protective headstrong men, a witch trying to teach and a whole lot of shenanigans of every variety. An absolute delight to read!" (Michelle on BookBub)

When I read, "... the first thing the blurb said about this book, "A tasteful tale of murder", I laughed so hard I thought I was going to choke on my tongue! I loved the first book in this series, and this added so much more to the story. When she said her life was a bloody mess, she wasn't joking! This was one wild ride, and I am so glad I get to be a part of it. Can't wait to see what comes next." (Exerhombre on BookBub)

Book III – Fangs for the Memories

"I giggled all the way through this book. Rebel Black is so adorably clueless in the romance department. Trying to handle an academy of delinquent but darling new vampires, plus her blackmailing hot vampire "employer" plus a sexy frenemy dhampyre security chief and a werewolf bodyguard who just wants to guard her body a bit closer? With an invisible bunny familiar who is no help at all? Then there's the theft, the murder (if you can murder an already dead vampire) and the prom from hell - this was a grin fest from page one..." (Melanie S. on BookBub)

"This series is hilarious. Nothing like a wicked witch (Rebel) educating the vampire delinquents and murder comes along, as well as a prom, a threat from the fiercest vampire of all, crazy family along with supernatural cops. You never know what you're going to be reading from page to page. It's one of those books I couldn't put down because I couldn't wait to see what would happen next..." (Loribeth16 on BookBub)

"Every time I read a book in this series, I'm just so tickled. Rebel, Onyx, Harvey, and all the other characters are just so much fun. In this latest there is theft, murder, and of course mayhem. Poor Rebel just can't seem to keep her vampires in line. ... I just love the way the author brings the characters and the setting to life, and I enjoy every second I'm immersed in the series including this book. I hope that the series goes on for many more books. Highly recommend ..." (PenKay on BookBub)

"I loved it. Highly entertaining - funny one minute infinitely sad the next. A total rollercoaster as Rebel tries to navigate her way through undead politics and murder." (DMA on BookBub)

"...I really like how the author builds on each book. The characters that are core to the story are written perfectly and new characters flow seamlessly into the story. I really would like to know what Alessandra has that he is blackmailing Rebel with... must be juicy! This is a very entertaining book..." (my2Doxie on BookBub)

"Who could imagine a school filled with teenage vampires. would be so much fun-to-read? They may be dangerous, but these characters are also endearing and irresistible... Sassy, clever, and absolutely unique. I can never get enough of this author's creations!" (Marianne on BookBub)

WHAT THE FANG?

FANGSTERS, BOOK 4

JO-ANN CARSON

BOOKS BY JO-ANN CARSON

Fangsters Series

Dial Witch Trilogy

The Perfect Brew Series

Mystic Keep Stories

A Ghost & Abby Mysteries

The Gambling Ghosts Series

Standalones

The Nanaimo Bar Christmas Mystery

Fangs for the Memories is a work of fiction. All names, characters, places, and incidents are the products of my imagination. Any resemblance to actual events, locales, or persons, living or dead, is entirely coincidental.

JRT Publications

ISBN 978-1-989031-64-3

Cover Design by Rebecca at Dream2Media

INTRODUCTION

WHAT THE FANG?

Who is stupid enough to pick on my vampires?

When a thief snatched the fang of one of my students, I had to stop them. Think about it. What's a vampire without a fang?

My name is Rebel Black. I'm the book-nerd-witch who runs Fangsters, the notorious school for delinquent, teenaged, night stalkers, housed in a Victorian bordello in Mystic Keep. It's a small town in the Pacific Northwest that looks picturesque and innocent, but my academy, filled with secrets, and more than its share of murders has been listed in the Supernatural Gazette as a ten on the Creepy Richter scale.

Trust me, I didn't choose this job. I'm being blackmailed by one of the most powerful vampires in all the realms, and until I devise a spell strong enough to stop him cold, I must do his bidding. But to be honest, teaching predators hasn't turned out to be as bad as you might expect. There's never a dull moment in the house of the rising dead. What can I say—predators grow on you.

Take Onyx, my head of security, for an example. He's a bit on the Dracula-gloomy side, but he's also breathtakingly handsome, and his deadly-dry wit keeps things lively.

Unfortunately, when I got the news about the stolen fang, Onyx was nowhere to be found. I suspect his disappearance has something to do with our lover's fight, but I can't worry about that right now. I must solve this tooth mess. No one steals from my bloodsuckers.

Will I find the Fang Hunter before more of my students lose their choppers? If I fail, and Fangsters is forced to close its doors, will my blackmailer carry out his threat and reveal my secret?

What the Fang is the fourth book in Fangsters, Jo-Ann Carson's Supernatural Suspense series. Witches, warlocks, werewolves, and monsters of all stripes are featured. It's a fast-paced mystery, with a slow-burn romance, and an edge of humor designed to entertain you. It can easily be read as a standalone.

CHAPTER ONE

Tonight, I would take my revenge. Make no mistake, witches, even the good ones, get even with people who cross them. That's why it's foolish to mess with a witch.

I stood alone in the parking lot outside Murphy's Bar in Seattle, imagining how sweet my revenge would taste. I knew Dakota—my lying, cheating, bastard of an ex-fiancé—would be inside schmoozing because that's what he did every Friday night after work. He'd be telling worn-out jokes and flirting with the waitresses.

The fog had grown so thick around me that I could barely make out the neon sign above the entrance. The acrid smell of beer turned my stomach. But nothing was going to stop me. Not tonight. I crept along the first row of parked cars, searching for Dakota's big truck. It was the kind of shiny toys men love to show off, as if the tread on the tires signifies their manhood.

Every few minutes when the bar's front door opened laughter spilled into the night. I ducked for cover whenever a figure appeared in the mist. The cloak-and-dagger aspect of my mission both thrilled and terrified me. Adrenalin rushed through my veins. My body tingled with anticipation. This was heady stuff for a book-nerd, like me who spent most of her Friday nights in a library.

But I wanted revenge more than I wanted my next breath. Dakota wronged me, and he would pay for it. I gave him my heart, and he broke it into a million pieces. I won't go over the tawdry details of how he ended our three-year betrothal, and how it tore apart my life plan. Let's just say the ending-to-end-all-endings involved a dominatrix with big hair, siren-red lips, and a whip.

That memory haunted me. Adding salt to my wounds, Dakota told everyone who would listen to him that his romp in the motel room was no big deal. "Boys will be boys," he said repeatedly, with a wink, or so I was told.

Boys will be boys. Hmph. To that I say, *Witches are witches.* He should know better than to cross a sorceress.

Dakota deserved all the pain I could unleash on him, and I planned on delivering it in ways that would hurt him most a bit at a time over the next year ... or ten. I had a revenge list.

Tonight, I wanted to hit him where it would hurt him most, right in the center of his oversized Goodyear tires. I knew some people labelled my need for revenge as immature, but I didn't care. I figured if I made Dakota suffer, my dignity would be restored and that in turn would help me move on. It's all about self-love and therapy.

In the distance, the sound of fog horns sliced through the dreariness of the night. The mist thickened wrapping itself around me. A rat scurried over my foot. I jumped—and slapped a hand over my mouth to muffle a scream.

I swallowed and took a deep breath. I needed to focus on my plan. I imagined Dakota crying as he called an Uber.

Hey, I could live with the memory of a rat to see that happen.

As I stalked through the second line of parked cars, I passed many sedans, jeeps, but I couldn't find Dakota's prized possession. I searched the lot a second time but found nothing. I bit my lip. He came to Murphy's Bar every Friday night after work. His truck had to be here somewhere.

Ten minutes later, I found it, a midnight-blue, fully loaded Ram that cost enough to feed a small country for a week. I pulled out my pocketknife and carefully slashed the rear tires. They were tougher than I expected, but I persevered. Of course, I could have used my magic to do the deed, but I wanted the visceral feeling of my revenge. The joy of it travelled through my skin right into my bones. I bent over the final tire with my blade.

A large hand clasped my shoulder. My stomach lurched, as I jolted and glanced up. An enormous man in a muscle shirt glared down at me. His nametag read *Arnold*.

"What have we here?" he barked, as he seized my hand that held the knife. I dropped my weapon.

"Ah ... I'm looking for my car."

He tilted his bald head to one side and spoke into a device strapped to his chest. "Got a wild one here."

I yearned to zap him with some of my witch fire, but I stopped myself. The Witch's Oath that I live by forbids me using my power for my own gain. Oh, holy hexen hell, I wanted to zap him.

And that is how I—a quiet, peace-loving, book nerd—ended up being charged with mischief and sent into a Seattle prison cell.

CHAPTER TWO

Being processed for jail didn't dampen the warm feeling of victory dancing through my veins. I had been successful in my mission. No matter what happened to me, I had ruined three of Dakota's beloved tires. He would be devastated. Nothing could diminish my smile.

"You're awful happy," said the heavy-set female cop, as she steered me by my elbow along the corridor to the holding cell. The woman must have spent hours in the gym.

I shrugged. "I'll pay the fine. Do the time. Whatever." I had already placed a call to my friend Eliza who lived nearby. She had promised to come as soon as she could to bail me out.

"Let me guess. You were getting back at your lover."

I huffed. "Ex," I corrected her. "And he's gonna be so upset. So deliciously upset. He might even cry for his mama."

"Mm hmm." The hard-faced cop shook her head. "Lady, you don't know what you've got yourself into."

I blinked. "A fine, I suppose."

"Hah. You don't get it. Have you thought about what's waiting for you down the hall, in this jail?" Her eyes hardened. "Tonight."

I shrugged. "It doesn't matter. I'll be out by morning."

Her furry left brow rose. "Yeah. If you last that long."

"Wh— Why wouldn't I?"

"Sweet cheeks, it's Friday night and there's a full moon. The holding cell is overflowing with ..." She looked me up and down. "Let's just say, people who don't look like you."

My throat thickened. "I don't get my own cell?"

She barked out a laugh. "Not a chance."

I swallowed hard at the sound of two women screaming at each other. There was enough rage in their voices to part the Pacific Ocean. One of them stopped mid-sentence to retch.

I slowed my pace.

The cop nodded. "Sounds like the regulars. You're just lucky it's not the third night of the full moon."

With a flick of her key pass, the lock on the cell clicked, and she opened the creaking door.

Now, I thought, would be a good time to use my magic and do a Houdini exit. I didn't deserve to be thrown into the loony bin. For that matter, I didn't deserve to be held accountable for anything I did to Dakota. He deserved a tire slashing and a lot more. I clenched my teeth and wished I could just use a teensy-weensy bit of magic to get me out of this jam.

With my chin raised, I stepped into the holding cell. It was about the size of a volleyball court. Twenty or so females mingled inside. Their sweat smelled like a party gone wrong.

Some sat on a bench along the back wall, but most stood. They all stared at me, the newbie. I aimed for an empty spot on the bench. As I moved, I glanced around at my roommates. The ladies, and I use that term loosely, ranged in age from sixteen to seventy. Every skin color and social subset was represented. The only common feature I could see was a sense of desperation.

I caught a whiff of demon blood, but otherwise, I discerned only norms. Angry, despairing, drunk, stoned, frustrated ... norms.

"What are you looking at?" snarled a pencil-thin woman in a white evening dress stained with blood.

"Nothing I said."

Before I could say more, her fist smashed into my face. I ducked, but not before I heard my nose crack. My skin tore apart with the impact of her punch. Blood flowed down my face and trickled into my mouth. Her ring scratched my skin as she withdrew her hand.

I lunged at her, but a s she deftly stepped aside laughing, I fell to the floor. I felt like a complete idiot, but a hand reached down for me and pulled me to my feet. As I stood, I watched the lady in the gown hit another, and then another. The whole cell broke out into a brawl.

CHAPTER THREE

Three hours later, bruised, battered, and bitchy, I drove home. I figured my problems for the night were over, thanks to Eliza posting bail for me. Turning up my radio to full-blast, I sang along with every break-up song they played on my favorite Country radio station, as I careened along the windy coastal road.

I had a posh apartment in Fangsters. It's my academy for vampire delinquents that sits on the outskirts of Mystic Keep, a cute coastal town. When the front door groaned open with its familiar Gothic-Horror melody, I felt confident the problems for the night had ended. I waved at the security cameras and slammed the door behind me with my foot. I was home!

But a chill skittered like a drunk spider up my spine. I froze. Everything inside the manor felt dead. Too dead, even for a place that housed vampires. But I was too tired to give it any more thought. I headed toward the grand staircase. My bed was calling my name.

With every step I climbed, an ominous, cold stillness seeped into my bones. I hesitated at the foot of the stairs and gripped the raven sculpture that stood upon the banister. Something was definitely wrong.

Normally, it being the weekend my students would be partying. Their music would filter up through the floor from the basement, which housed their residence, the casino would be hopping, and stray vampires would be wandering about. But I couldn't hear any music.

I shook my head. I shouldn't be concerned. After all there is no such thing as *normal* in a school for teenage vampires. I had to stop looking for it.

My head ached. Hex it, I told myself, I'll worry tomorrow. My limbs felt heavy as I climbed the stairs to my apartment on the top floor. My four-poster bed awaited me with deliciously soft, Egyptian-cotton sheets. When I'd lived on my own, I could never afford such luxury, but my blackmailer, the infamous Alessandro from Amsterdam, made my personal space comfortable. I stripped naked and slid between the sheets with a sigh of relief. Tomorrow would be a new day.

Settling my head on the pillow, I reminded myself that the night had not been a complete failure. I had slit three of Dakota's tires. I smiled at the thought of his face when he looked at them, and I dozed off.

"Long night, darlin'?" asked a voice with a Texan accent.

I groaned and opened my eyes. Harvey, my familiar who happens to be a rabbit had decided to appear. He sat cross-legged in a recliner in the corner of my room.

Why do I have to have a familiar who asks stupid questions, I wondered.

"I'm just part of your weird and wonderful life, darlin'," he replied, because he could hear my thoughts.

I closed my eyes tightly. My mom told me I got a bunny

because I'm allergic to cats and Harvey was the universe's solution. My sisters blame my father, a mysterious, fae prince no one other than my mother has ever met. I think it's because the Fates needed a good laugh.

"I do make you laugh," Harvey said wiggling his brows.

My heart stuttered. While he was not like other familiars, he was mine, and I treasured him. Being shy, he preferred to remain invisible to others, which is awkward, but, on the plus side, he likes to cuddle with me when I read, and his deep cowboy voice calms my nerves.

He grinned as he listened to my thoughts. "You've had an interesting evening, darlin'."

"Mission accomplished," I mumbled. Who knew being a bad girl could be so exhausting? My eyes closed and I drifted off into a wonderful fantasy about a pirate king who needed a librarian.

I AWOKE from a deep sleep to the familiar scent of vampire. I felt as if the devil himself had grabbed my heart and squeezed the life out of me.

I opened one eye. Of course, it was Alessandro, one of the most powerful vampires in all the realms. Standing beside my bed, he loomed over me.

"Go away," I said, and pulled a pillow over my head.

He removed the pillow with one of his gigantic hands and tossed it into the air. "I heard you were a bad girl tonight."

Of course, he'd heard. I sat up and took him in.

The night predator had thick mahogany-brown hair that flowed in waves to his broad shoulders. Dark brown eyes dominated his ruggedly handsome face. His square jaw had just the right amount of scruff on it to make a woman sigh, and his full lips held a bad-boy grin. Alessandro was sexier than any man ought to be. I exhaled slowly. His presence filled my bedroom with a delicious sense of danger. Unfortunately for me, he was stone-cold-dead—and in a twisted way, my brother.

I saluted him. “I might have been in trouble, but I’m home now.”

“Mm. I like it when good girls act bad.” He hesitated a beat because immortals never talk fast. “And, I would normally enjoy hearing all the juicy details of your escapade, but not tonight.” He made a vampire guttural sound that made me wince.

“I’m exhausted, Alessandro, and it’s almost dawn. Can’t you just go away for now?”

He shook his head.

I groaned. “Send me a message. I promise you I’ll respond in the morning.”

“Nuh uh.” He lowered his body to sit on the edge of my bed. “We need to talk. Now.”

I would have said no, if I could, but he was the one person in all the realms I could not say no to. “Not without coffee,” I muttered.

“There’s no time.”

No time for coffee? I straightened my back and slowly gained my bearings. My vampire brother had never denied me caffeine. He wasn’t that mean. “What’s wrong?” I asked. Instinctively I grabbed for my Fae grandmother’s pendant that I wore around my neck for good luck. This news had to be bad.

“One of our students was attacked by a Fang Hunter.”

“What?” Now I was fully awake. One of *my* students

attacked! “Where’s Onyx?” He was the dhamphyre who took care of the academy’s security.

“Onyx is gone.”

“Gone?” I squinted. I’d only left the building for one day and part of one night. How could this have happened?

Alessandro growled, and the low timber of his predator grumble rolled through the room echoing off the walls. The bone-chilling sound made my chest tighten and my blood run cold. The big guy was a lot more upset than I thought.

“It’s not like him to leave us,” I said pulling my quilt tighter around my body.

“I have been told the two of you had a fight.” His predator eyes lasered into mine.

I blinked. “We always fight. You know that.”

“But this one ...” He arched a manly brow. “... was loud enough that the whole residence heard you.”

I exhaled slowly. “He made me mad.” Onyx always made me mad.

“Mm hmm.”

“You know how witches get when we’re angry.” I bit my lip and tried to make sense of it all. “Do you really think that’s why he left?” I scrunched my face. “That doesn’t sound like Onyx.”

The vampire shrugged.

“He’s a tough guy,” I continued, “and ... trust me, my opinions don’t matter to him.”

Alessandro scoffed. “Men don’t always say what they mean, Rebel. You need to learn that.”

I shook my head. I wasn’t about to discuss my man problems with a dead one who was blackmailing me. “Have you tried looking for Onyx?”

“What do you think? I tried to contact him in every

possible way. Onyx is gone, and you need to stop the Fang Hunter on your own."

"Me?"

"Yes, you."

"But I'm a bibliophile, not a detective."

He leaned closer. The coppery scent of human blood dangled on his breath. "Do I need to remind you what is at stake for you?"

I groaned. Alessandro knew my deepest, darkest secret. If people found out what I had done, I would be destroyed. He leveraged this knowledge to get me to start the academy for his wayward progeny and continued to hold it over me so that I would do his bidding.

During his long undead life, Alessandro had collected and traded many people's secrets using them for his own purposes. It was like a hobby for him, and one had made him powerful and rich. I understood that, but I sure didn't like him holding my life in his hands.

"Alessandro, you can't—"

His jaw hardened for a beat, and then he spoke in his solemn voice. "If you don't eliminate this threat to the students, I will consider our contract terminated." His jaw firmed. "You know what that means. I will tell everyone your secret."

I nodded, too afraid to trust my voice.

"Rebel?"

"How can I?" My mind reeled at the prospect of having to find the villain on my own. "Can I go into the tunnels?" Alessandro had taken over an underground network of passageways and caverns created by smugglers in the nineteenth centuries to move black market tobacco, booze, and drugs from the harbor into the town. It hadn't been used in decades, but his band of night creatures had renovated it to suit their needs.

It's how the vampires got around town, how they escaped the sun, and where they fed most of the time. The student and staff residences had been built down there as well. I had been asking for a tour since we opened the academy but had been denied each time I asked.

"No, not now," he said, and then in almost a whisper, "Not ever."

"Alessandro!"

"No, Rebel. The world below the academy is not a place for mortal beings."

"But that's where the fang was taken. How do you expect me to solve this case when I can't even look at the scene of the crime?"

He shrugged. "Talk to the students and staff. They live down there. They will give you all the information you need."

"But if I could just see—"

"No." He folded his arms. His predator stare grew so intense I thought I might sizzle beneath it. "Under no circumstances are you to step below the ground level of the academy."

I swallowed. "Okay. I will respect your boundaries."

"And?" he said in a gravelly voice that raked my senses.

"I will find the Fang Hunter," I said.

"Forty-eight hours." Alessandro stood. "I'll give you forty-eight hours. You work best on a timeline. Get this done."

"Impossible."

He tilted his head. "Thirty-six then."

CHAPTER FOUR

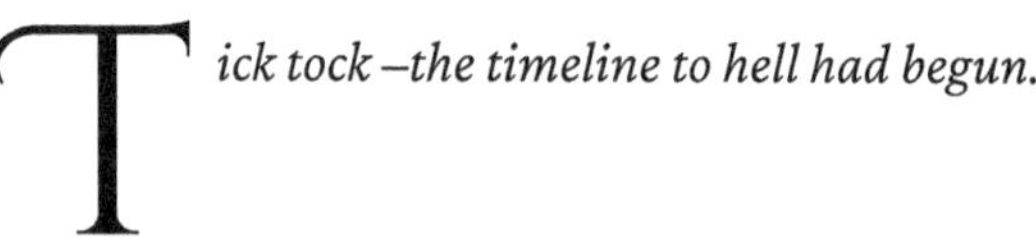

Tick tock –the timeline to hell had begun.

The next morning after I had consumed a pot of coffee, I descended to my office on Fangsters' ground floor and penned a to-do list. My body still hurt from the big brawl at the joint, but I didn't have time to worry about my personal pain. More important things were going on in my world. I had become a tooth fairy—well, more like a fang fairy. Whatever. I had to protect Fangsters from a Fang Hunter. They were my students, whatever their specie, and no one was going to hurt them on my watch.

To-Do List

1 *Contact a lawyer in case Dakota presses criminal charges.*

2 *Have René (our resident genius about everything) crack* *the CCTV data at Murphy's Bar and send me the footage of Dakota finding his flat tires. A woman has to have some fun in her day.*

3 *Send Onyx a ~~warm~~ ~~friendly~~ ~~cryptic~~ non-apologetic apology message. Tell him I ~~want~~ need him back to deal with a security issue. Wave an olive branch with the condition he stay out of my private life.*

4 *Wait twenty minutes for a reply and then send an official academy request to Onyx demanding his assistance, stating there is no one better—anywhere in the realm—to neutralize a Fang Hunter. (I gagged as I wrote this sentence.)*

6 *Talk to the police.*

7 *Get one of my sisters to brew a pain-killing potion for my killer of a headache before I kill someone.*

Where the hex was Onyx? He drove me crazy in so many ways, but I needed him. I thought about how angry he looked when I used my magic to throw him across the room. I could still remember the sound of his body hitting the wall. He had walked off in a huff, but I thought we would get over it. Maybe I was wrong about that. Maybe, the fanged one had sensitive feelings. Is that what Alessandro had tried to tell me?

I closed my eyes as I thought of him. Onyx was a super-hot guy. He looked like Ryan Reynolds with bangs—and fangs. Being a dhamphyre—that is a predator with a vampire father and mortal mother—he lived in an in-between world. He wasn't dead or immortal, but he would live a very long life and he had some vampire powers. Daylight didn't bother him, and his diet included food from all the realms as well as blood. Understanding both the mortal and immortal cultures he was the perfect security man for the academy and that's why Alessandro had chosen him, or at least that's what I figured. But he wasn't the perfect housemate for me. We fought a lot.

Needing to get on with playing detective, I read my to-do list out loud. Had I left anything out?

Harvey shrugged and said nothing, which said a lot.

The list felt inadequate. I grumbled. This was not a day I looked forward to living in the house of the undead.

Harvey, who lounged in a chair in the corner of my office, cleared his throat. "Please, don't think that. You know what happens when you do."

"Things get worse." I smiled grimly. "I know I'm tempting the Fates. But things can't possibly get worse this time."

A raucous *caw* drew my attention to my open window. *The* raven had returned. When I looked his way, he made a clucking sound.

"Well, good morning to you too, my friend." I saw him every day, sometimes at my bedroom window and sometimes here in my office. I figured he was hungry, so I left him breadcrumbs on little dishes.

"But he doesn't eat them," said Harvey, sounding as smug as ever. "May I remind you ravens are known for pecking out the eyes of dying men?"

"So, you tell me." Every day.

"I can show you pictures," Harvey added.

"Stop glaring at him. Maybe he'll start eating when he feels more comfortable with us."

"You want to train a wild bird of prey?

"No, that's not it. I just think it's hospitable to offer food to a guest."

"Hmm. Cuz training men is something you're so good

at." Harvey muttered his words with his southern drawl, but I heard them well enough.

And I laughed. "Maybe I should try cookies instead of bread?

"How about cake?"

"There's an idea."

"I was joking."

I scoffed.

Someone pounded on the academy's front door, and my heart skipped a beat. Who would be visiting me in the daylight?

I exhaled slowly. "You better not be right about things getting worse," I said to Harvey.

I got up, but before I could take a step, I heard the front door crash open. A second later my office door smashed into the wall. Two big men strode towards me with fire in their eyes. With a sigh, I sat down and folded my hands on my lap.

Of course, it would be them. Only family would disturb my peace at—I glanced at the clock on my phone—six in the morning. My two brothers-in-laws marched to my desk as if the mahogany piece of furniture was an enemy of the state to be seized. They stared down their official noses at me. If I didn't love them, I might have squirmed. But I knew their growls to be worse than their bites, at least as far as I was concerned.

On the right stood Gavin McGee, my sister Jane's werewolf mate. He was the norm police chief in Mystic Keep, a big guy built to handle trouble. The glint in his eye made me cringe. Clearly, he considered me to be a problem. No one messed with the peace in his small town. His official blue uniform fit snugly over his muscular frame but didn't hide his scuffed cowboy boots. He growled loud enough to shake my teaching license hanging on the wall behind me.

"Good morning, to you too," I said.

Standing to his left, Donovan O'Reilly quirked a black brow. A warlock warrior with a legendary reputation, he had married my oldest sister, Merlina. He tossed back his magical cloak over his shoulder, revealing a lean, hard body fitted with top-of-the-line battle gear. No doubt this was an instinctual move he used to intimidate people he interrogated, but it did little to impress me. I had heard him coo to his baby son a few nights ago and knew just how soft a heart hid beneath the Kevlar gear.

Donovan's Irish blue eyes sizzled with anger. "Rebel! This place is trouble."

"And so are you two," I said.

I glanced from one to the other and smiled. "As a matter of fact, I was just about to call you." I figured that would make them feel better, as they were always telling me I should rely on them.

"There's been nothing but problems since *this place* opened," said Gavin. His nose wiggled as if he picked up a scent.

"Ah come on. That's not completely true," I said. While there was never a dull night in my school for delinquent vampires, it wasn't the only source of mayhem. I cleared my throat. "We all know the real truth. There was unrest in Mystic Keep before I came to town. Ever since my great aunt Ophelia made it a haven for magic folk trouble has stirred. My school is just a ... touch of whip cream on that sundae."

Donovan pinched the bridge of his nose. "We were told there's been an incident here."

"Who contacted you?"

"It was an anonymous tip," said Gavin, his gaze drifted to the window and whipped back to me. "But since your phone is off, we decided to pay you a personal visit."

They both stared at me.

I looked past them at Harvey, still sitting in the corner. He shrugged.

"Perhaps you would like to sit down for this," I said as I opened the file on my ink blotter.

Donovan sat on the edge of my desk with a grumble. Gavin strolled to the window and stared outside.

"I was away for one day and one night," I said. "When I came back..." I stopped to take a deep breath. "I found this file folder on my desk." I didn't tell them about Alessandro visiting me in the night because that would raise their hackles. The less they knew about my relationship with him, the better. They knew Alessandro bankrolled Fangsters, but they didn't know he'd blackmailed me to run it.

"Where did you go?" muttered Gavin.

I huffed. "Seattle, not that it matters."

"Is that where you got the black eye?" asked Donovan.

Dang it all, I thought my witch charm hid the bruises, but warlocks have sharp eyes that can see below all of that. It's as if they smell wounds. "That's not important right now." I waved my hand in the air.

"Seattle, eh." Gavin glanced my way. "Isn't that where the Ass Hat lives?" *Ass Hat* was Gavin's pet name for Dakota. One of the many reasons I loved the werewolf.

"Yeah."

Donovan stiffened. "He hit you?"

"No. No. I got this from a hysterical woman in the joint. Can we get back to business?"

Gavin snickered. "The joint? Do you mean jail? You?"

Donovan leaned toward me and sniffed. "She tells the truth."

Gavin pulled out his phone and started tapping.

I cleared my throat. "As I said, my trip is not important."

Donovan tucked a lock of hair behind my ear. "It's a real shiner, honey."

"Hah," said Gavin. "Here's the truth. Our dear little sister was arrested last night for mischief. Apparently, she was caught slitting tires in the parking lot of Murphy's Bar."

Donovan chuckled. "My, my, Rebel, you've been naughty. Hanging around vampires is turning you ... wicked."

I closed my eyes. My cheeks burned. "Can we talk business?"

Gavin kept tapping on his phone. "Her charges are pending, but she was supposed to appear in a Seattle court this morning. What do you think, Donovan? Shall we report her?"

"An escapee? Oh, this is getting even better. Wait until I tell Merlina."

"No!" I jumped up and planted my fists on my hips. "You need to listen to me. I need help."

"You're a mild-mannered witch running a school for gangsters who bite. Why would you need help?" said Donovan with a sly smile.

Then it happened. I couldn't help myself. I'm not that powerful a sorceress, but when I get angry, really angry, energy flows out of my body and effects the electric grid. It's just a thing that happens, and I can't control it. The lights in my office flashed on and off.

Gavin laughed. "Yup, she's in trouble." He returned to my desk and folded his body into a guest chair to face me.

Donovan eased himself into the other chair. "Tell us." He used his authoritarian voice, the one that had led supernatural armies into battle.

My stomach twisted. "One of my students was assaulted."

"While you were in the clinker?" asked Gavin.

"Where was Onyx?" Donovan mused.

I sighed. "Here's the thing ... Onyx is gone, and I need to fix a missing fang problem. I can't talk to any of the vampires until dark. So maybe you guys can help me."

"Hmm," they grumbled in unison like a boy-band chorus. "You have a fang problem?"

"Yes. There's a Fang Hunter in town. All the information I have is in this file," I explained.

CHAPTER FIVE

Before I could look inside the file, Norman, my norm janitor tapped on my open office door and entered with a tray of coffee. He was a middle-aged man with wispy salt and pepper hair that he combed over his bald spot. He had a sizable paunch and dressed in a blue flannel shirt and jeans. My brothers glared at him for the intrusion.

"Don't bite me," he said. That was his standard line. It usually worked well, but these guys were a hard audience.

They shook their heads in disbelief.

I bit back a laugh. "Thanks, Norm."

As he put the tray down on my desk, the three ceramic mugs rattled. Norm glanced at the file. "I see you're busy. I'll leave you to it."

When the door clicked behind Norm, Gavin's brow furrowed. "Who is that guy?"

"The janitor. Onyx hired him weeks ago."

"Since when does a janitor deliver coffee?" asked Donovan.

"And how did he know how many mugs to bring?" added Gavin.

"Hey, stop complaining. I trust him. And, its coffee," I poured the first cup and gave it to Gavin. "Norm has grown protective of me during the day because the vampires are all resting. He keeps an eye on any visitors coming or going. It's sweet, really." Though I guessed he was paid to make reports to Alessandro.

Gavin grunted.

"Take the coffee." I handed him a cup. "Whatever's in this file will be easier to face with caffeine."

Gavin examined his mug. It was one of my favorites, with the words *Vampires Suck* written in red text that dripped as if it were blood. A faint smile lightened his expression as he studied the slogan. He took a gulp. "Tell us about the Fang Hunter."

Donovan groaned but didn't refuse the coffee I handed to him. It was in a red mug, with a black silhouette of Dracula dancing across the words, *The Fangdango*.

I lifted my mug in a silent toast and took a sip. Pure heaven. Norm had been bringing me coffee every morning since he started working in the academy. We'd swap stories. He would tell me about the old days when he was an engineer on the trains, or of his many travels to the Arctic. Since one man couldn't experience that much adventure in one lifetime, I doubted all his tales were true, but I didn't care how much he exaggerated. I enjoyed his tales. They had become a thing that made living in the house of the rising dead feel more normal. The saying on my cup was *Good to the last bite*. I smiled and took another sip.

Gavin got up, locked my office door, and returned to his seat. "So, what's in the file?"

"A summary report and a flash drive."

Donovan nodded. "Read it."

"*Incident Report, filed by René @ sunrise.*" I stopped. "You remember René, right?"

"He's the brainy one," said Gavin. "With the French accent that makes women purr."

Donovan nodded. "The savant who runs a gambling business. I recall you saying it was motivational for him to have his own gig, but I think he's skirting a lot of inter-realm laws." He grimaced. "Yeah, we know all about René."

I didn't like his tone, so I stopped to take a long drink of my coffee just to annoy him. It burned my tongue. I continued to read.

"Observations*: When we arose at sunset, Xiu, who rests next to me, was missing a fang. It had been pulled.*

Victim*: Xiu, thirty-year-old vampire of Chinese descent, appears sixteen, slim, healthy, smart—maybe too smart. Sired by Alessandro, he is always in trouble with the norms. His last mistake was passing counterfeit one-hundred-dollar bills to a gang of mobsters in Chicago. They chained him to a cement wall in a duplex and took wagers on how long he could last without blood. Alessandro rescued him and brought him here.*

Investigation*: Terror spread quickly below ground. Someone had come into our dorm, assaulted Xiu, and escaped seemingly unnoticed. Unable to locate Onyx or Rebel, I took over the role of head of security. I interviewed all the students and faculty. You can find recordings of the interviews on the thumb drive.*

Summation*: There were no visitors staying in the residences. The doors were locked and secured by Onyx's mechanical devices and Rebel's spells. No stranger should have been able to come in, do the crime, and leave. But someone did.*

It's a locked casket case.

Suspects:

A mage did it. Why? Because they hate us. We know they have ***motivation****. Their magic would be their* ***means****. But did they have the* ***opportunity****? We need to find out what they were up to that night.*

Claudia, the newbie vamp, did it. She has been with us for forty-eight hours and is yet to speak to anyone. She refused to be interviewed. Does she know something?

A stranger did it. The unknown factor needs to be considered. Has a Fang Hunter come to town and infiltrated our security system?"

I put down René's report and picked up my coffee.

Donovan pinched the bridge of his nose. "Interesting," he mumbled.

"But?" asked Gavin.

"No one is dying here," said Donovan with a huff. "I've got a Troll situation happening in the river quarter. If I can't solve Junker's murder, which happened yesterday, a war will break out between two of the dominant families, and more trolls will die. I need to be there."

My gut twisted. Since when did Trolls rate higher than Vamps? Since always, in this town. I sighed. "I understand," I said, but I didn't.

"I came to make sure you were all right." Donovan plunked his empty cup on the tray with a decisive thump. "And quite frankly, I don't give a damn about a missing fang."

"Hmm," grumbled Gavin.

Donovan stood. "I trust the two of you will sort this out." He rotated his hands and a flaming portal appeared in the space behind him.

"Wait," I said.

He cocked a brow, as the flames burned behind him, backlighting him with flickering, blue light.

"Before you go … tell me what you know about Fang Hunters."

Donovan winced.

"Please. It will save us time," I added. He would know more about them than anyone in town.

The Irish warlock firmed his jaw. "Vampire fangs are traded on black markets in all the nine realms. They are used in magic spells and norm medicines. While many have tried their pliers at vamp hunting, most have not lived to tell the tale. The Vampire Brotherhood takes care of them."

His Adam's apple went up and down, and I imagined horrific images of torture and death at the hands of angry vampires.

"Still," he continued after a moment, "there's a lot of money in fangs, and cash makes desperate people do desperate things." Without waiting for a reply, he turned and strode through his flaming portal.

Gavin poured himself another cup of coffee. "So, tell me, why did Onyx leave?" He waited a beat. "What did you do to him?"

There wasn't coffee strong enough anywhere in the world, for me to face that question. "It doesn't matter. He's gone, and we need a plan."

CHAPTER SIX

Tick Tock –30 hours left to fix my fang problem.

After an hour of discussion, Gavin and I came up with a plan, which I had no intention of following. I pretended to agree with his ideas just to get him out of my office. He kissed me on the cheek before he left, and the scent of alpha wolf enveloped me like a warm hug on a cold morning.

"Remember the plan," he said.

I hid my feelings behind a forced smile, and probably looked constipated as all hex. It was all too much. Where the hex was Onyx? He'd left me with Gavin's man-plan to fix everything, and a fang crisis I had no idea how to solve. "Of course," I said to the werewolf in a demure voice. "I can do my part."

His denim-blue eyes narrowed. "Rebecca?"

"I'll do my best." And I would. I wasn't lying about that part. I always do my best.

"Mm hmm." His phone dinged before he could say more.

"You better get that," I said. "Your dings are important. I'm good, here. You go do you." I waved him out.

He left, but not before he gave me another suspicious glare.

I leaned back in my chair and exhaled slowly. It was time to devise my own scheme.

"That's my darlin'," said Harvey, nodding his approval from his chair in the corner.

"Can you believe Gavin! His plan is for him to take over and do all the investigating, while I sit here at my desk. As if!" I looked down at the suspect list. This is my school, and I will take care of things. "I'm going to question the mages. They're always causing us trouble."

"The mages!" Harvey repeated slowly. "I feel a list coming on." He pressed his paw to his forehead, as if he were a southern belle about to have a fainting spell.

"René listed them as the number one suspect."

"Mages?" Harvey's whiskers twitched.

"You already said that. What's your point?"

Harvey rolled his eyes. "Do I need to remind you, that you have history with them?"

"All the more reason to check them out."

"They twitter, X or whatever, about you every day."

I shrugged.

"They hold demonstrations on our grounds." Harvey pointed to the window. "They even set bombs."

"Protest is legal in a democracy." I said.

"Face it, darlin'. They have it in for your whole family."

I nodded. "Well, yes, but what would a small town be without a family feud or two."

Harvey's nose crinkled. "And ... they have magic."

My fingers trembled. "You're not helping."

An hour later, decked in black yoga pants, a black turtle,

and a black cape, I sauntered down Main Street toward the mage headquarters housed in a dilapidated warehouse at the north end. I had tied my hair back into a low ponytail, pulled the hood of my cloak over my head, and shadowed my jaw with makeup so I appeared to have facial scruff. Large Harry Potter glasses completed my disguise as a young mage. The only thing I lacked was a large pendant with the gold emblem of their guild on it. I figured I'd steal one the first chance I got.

It didn't take me long to arrive at the front door of the Mage Guild. It was an ugly brick albatross of a building, created during the height of the industrial revolution, a time when efficiency far outweighed aesthetics. To my mind, it was an eyesore in the quaint seaside town.

The Guild headquarters had a storied past. It had once been owned by a successful yuppie who turned it into a fleece making factory. After five successful years, the man's tech-stocks took a dive, and he jumped from the top floor. Before him, the structure had been a youth hostel. Countless backpackers exploring the beauty of the Pacific Northwest coast visited there until a guest started a fire. There were several casualties. That owner collected the insurance money and ran saying the place had too many ghosts for him. Or so goes the local legends. The place was not only ugly, but it also had bad mojo. When I heard the Mage Guild bought it, I grinned from ear to ear.

I don't have anything against mages, per se. Some of them are my friends. Well, I have coffee with one ... maybe once a year, standing up.

It's the local Guild, that's the problem. They meddle in everyone's business, as if they have the right to interfere and manipulate the lives of others, as if they are superior, as if they know what's best. Did I mention they were mostly men and that they hate witches? That too, is a problem.

The red brick walls appeared stained by salt and weather. They made the building look old and neglected. The air around it reeked of mages—a disgusting mixture of garlic, body odor, and weak magic.

I readied my magical power allowing it to rise to my fingertips. If the mages recognized me as an outsider, they'd act defensively, so I needed to be ready for that. I wasn't sure what they would do, but it wouldn't be nice. While the average mage possessed no more power than I did, a group could take me down in an instant. My witch senses warned me that there were at least twenty roaming inside the meeting house.

I lifted my chin and took a deep breath as I entered their domain. Unfortunately, my plan didn't go any farther than opening the door. I trusted luck and the universe for the rest. I swallowed. Maybe my plan wasn't so great. Who did I think I was? Indiana Jones with a broom?

I exhaled slowly as I gazed around the rectangular space. Office cubicles lined two sides of the room leaving a large empty area in the middle, and a food station at one end. The smell of mage sorcery and stale coffee hung in the air. A group of nine stood in a circle around a cauldron in the middle chanting in an ancient language. Others worked in their cubicles. A few lounged-on sofas near the food chatting. I spied a staircase beside them and a rear exit door I could use to escape. A wise witch always knows how to skedaddle.

A large banner hung on the back wall: Mage Guild of Mystic Keep. In us, we trust.

Humble as always, I thought.

As no one looked my way, I walked slowly along the

side of a bank of cubicles filled with mages working on laptops. Probably messaging, I thought. Not one of them looked up. But then, there were enough cameras on the walls and ceilings to protect Fort Knox.

I sucked on my lower lip. My gut swirled with acid. If the mages hid a secret, it probably wouldn't be in their front room. Maybe there would be private offices with locked safes upstairs or in the basement.

"Stop! Who goes there?" A man's voice came from behind me.

Without hesitation, I walked on, as if he couldn't possibly be talking to me, but the hair on the nape of my neck stood on end.

"I said stop!" The man barked. "Where is your pendant?"

I winced as a bony hand grabbed my bicep. He squeezed hard and spun me around. I found myself face to face with Egor Lugnut, the leader of the Guild whose official title was Sir Regal, Honor of Mages. In my family, we called him the Head Twit.

His sallow complexion looked even paler than I remembered it to be, and his beady eyes appeared ready to jump out of his face and attack me on their own. The last time I saw him he had tried to blow up my academy, so saying we had history put it mildly.

"I smell witch!" he said. He stared down his nose at me. "A bitch of a witch."

CHAPTER SEVEN

"Wait. I can explain," I said.

"Talk. Talk. Talk. That's all you witches do," Lugnut grumbled. Dandruff flecked his black mage's cloak that hung over his rotund body. The smell of garlic and his personal body odor hung in the air around him like a cloud.

"Yes, witches talk. That's because we have something to say."

He grunted, expelling more of his personal stench. I guess I was somewhat to blame for that. After I opened the vampire academy in Mystic Keep, the mages started adding garlic to every one of their meals. Mages in every realm tended to be on the quirky side, but our local ones really took the golden cauldron on paranoia.

I wrinkled my nose. "Sir Regal—Whatever." I huffed. "I expect as a fellow sorcerer and guest in your establishment to be treated with dignity."

Lugnut twisted his mouth. "Why? Why are you here, witch?"

"I'm hot on the bloody trail of a Fang Hunter."

He released my arm and straightened his back. “Here? Here?”

“Your guild, sir, is well known through all the realms, as a welcoming place for magic folk.” I lied.

He blinked twice.

“So,” I continued, “I thought a stranger might try to hide amongst you, kind supernatural souls.”

Lugnut scratched his chubby chin making his jowls wobble. “Yes. Yes. We are a fine guild.”

My shoulders relaxed. “Well?” I said. “Have you seen anyone suspicious lurking around?”

“A fang ... A Fang Hunter, you say?”

I tried to keep a straight face. How long does it take to bring a mage up to speed? “Yes, Sir Regal ... a Fang Hunter. I’m told there’s a lucrative trade in vampire fangs on the black market.”

“Indeed. Indeed.”

I nodded. “One of my students was attacked in his ... sleep.”

Lugnut’s eyes widened. “You ...” A small smile crept onto his face. “You don’t say.”

I grumbled to bring him back to earth. “It’s terrible. A vampire can’t survive without their fangs, and apparently false ones don’t work as well.”

The mage nodded. “I ... I see.” He took a deep breath. “I ... I will check with our security team and have them review our guest book and CCTV footage. But ... But I haven’t seen anyone strange.” He hesitated. “Other than you.”

“I’m not strange.”

“Hmm.”

“Where were you last night?” I asked him in a casual tone.

The line between his eyes deepened, and he folded his arms. "Surely … Surely you don't suspect me?"

You bet your sweet-mage ass I do, I thought, but I didn't say that. "Look, Sir Regal, you either tell me, or you tell Donovan and Gavin. We're trying to eliminate all the people we know. It's a standard procedure thing amongst detectives."

His face blanched at the sound of my brothers' names.

"Well?" I asked.

He huffed, and more garlic stench floated my way.

I coughed.

"After … After sunset … I was here watching a movie with the others until ten, and then we played Euchre until midnight. I'm sure that will all be on the CCTV tapes, which I will send to you."

"Thank you. And after midnight?"

"I … I went to my room upstairs, read for a while, and fell asleep. I woke at sunrise."

Another mage, I recognized as his second-in-command, stepped forward. "I was here. What the grand master says is true."

I exhaled slowly. "Do you have any idea of who the Fang Hunter could be?"

The two mages glanced at each other.

"Not everyone likes vampires in this town," said the second-in-command.

"Tell me something I don't know." I firmed my lips. "But the locals are getting used to them. I don't think it's a local."

"A … A vampire did it." Lugnut spoke with certainty. "They … They enjoy hurting others, you know."

I bit my top lip to stop myself from cursing. After a moment, I answered him. "You have my number. Please forward me footage from your cameras last night and let me know if you learn anything about the Fang Hunter."

Lugnut squinted. "You ... you're not getting off that easy."

I blinked. The two mages moved closer to me. I felt like a slice of bologna in a cheap cafeteria sandwich, squished between the bread and slimy butter. I pulled my protective magic around me. The others in the room stood and moved towards us.

"She has to walk the walk," said someone in the back of the room. I hadn't realized until that moment that all the mages in the room must have stopped what they were doing to listen in to our conversation. Hexen hell!

"The walk," repeated another.

"Walk. Walk. Walk."

If I wasn't gripped by terror, I might have found their chanting humorous. But there was nothing funny about their walk of shame. I had heard stories about it. It was notorious, as in notoriously bad.

"Make her do it," said another cloaked mage closing in on me. His words echoed in the hall.

"Walk. Walk. Walk." The chant continued. They raised their voices louder, and the whole room shook with their enthusiasm. They thumped their staffs as they circled me. It was like being in the center of a really bad musical. "Walk. Walk. Walk" *Thump. Thump. Thump*. "Walk. Walk. Walk." *Thump. Thump. Thump.* As their energy grew, a sense of foreboding pushed in on my senses.

I fought the trembling in my body, but to no avail. Sweat trickled down my spine. My chest tightened to the point I could hardly breathe, and an icy-cold weight settled in the pit of my stomach. I had heard about the mage's walk of shame, but never actually witnessed it.

Lugnut's beady eyes burned into mine. "I proclaim ..."

The group fell silent.

"That Rebel Black of the Black Magnolia witch coven deserves punishment. She trespassed on our sacred space, and she must pay for her foolishness."

"Wait. No. I'm here to protect others. You can't—"

His hand rose, and a mage spell resonated through the room. Before I could say another word, my clothes flew off my body. I stood bare-naked in front of him. My enchantress powers were nothing against the collective energy of the mage guild.

Nonetheless I tried to fight back. As tears of frustration, anger, and shame ran down my face, I called on my magic. I pleaded with the universe. I cursed the ground Lugnut stood on. This was not justice.

My pleas and curses were drowned in the swamp of their spells. I mentally called on my sisters for help, but I didn't think they would hear me, and even if they did, they wouldn't be able to get to me in time. I was truly done for.

I considered trying to cover my private parts, but I only had two hands. Raw anger stilled my edginess. I took a deep breath and stood tall. Screw this, I thought. I firmed my lips and stopped crying. Whatever they had in mind, I would endure it, and someday I would get my payback. Someday. I do love payback.

Lugnut's brow furrowed at the change in my demeanor. "You are a proud little witch. That's your problem, Rebel Black. You are too proud."

"Proud? I'm not the bully in the room." I spit out my words. I could see by the way he flinched, I hit my mark.

"Normally we would make you walk around the chamber three times. But for you ..."

"More. More. More." The mages had not lost their voices.

"For you, it will be once, a warning that you should never ever underestimate The Mage Guild of Mystic Keep. And ... and ... you should never enter our domain without an invitation."

I tossed my hair back and walked in the direction he pointed. Sometimes a witch has to do what a witch has to do. I was there to protect my students. I could do this for them. I had to do this.

But my sheer, gut-wrenching humiliation could not be contained. Tears flowed down my cheeks, as I placed one foot in front of the other. The hungry eyes of the mages devoured my nakedness. I had never felt so exposed, so alone, or so shamed. To make matters worse, the cold air in the room hardened my nipples. Could anything be crueler than this walk? The fifty yards I traversed felt like fifty freaking miles.

When I returned to my starting point, my clothes magically returned to my body smelling slightly of mage breath. I wiped the remnants of my tears from my face with the back of my hand and faced Lugnut. "Now what?"

"You ... You may go."

I considered threatening him, but I didn't want more trouble. Any dispute I took to the town's magic council would favor the mages. I had violated their space without permission. I had done wrong. I took a deep breath. "Let me know if you hear anything about the Fang Hunter," I said.

"Of course," replied Lugnut. His smug smile revealed blackened teeth.

That merciless grin pushed me one inch too far. I stepped closer to him, so that only he could hear my voice. "I will get you back for this. Someday. Somewhere. I will take my revenge. You are a marked man, Lugnut. Mark my words, I Rebel Black of the Black Magnolia coven have made you a marked man." I vanished in a puff of pink smoke scented with cotton candy to annoy the group. Using my magic to this extent would give me a terrible migraine, but I desperately wanted to show them I had power.

"Witch!" Lugnut hissed through the mist.

CHAPTER EIGHT

Tick Tock – 26 hours remaining to stop the Fang Hunter.

As I teleported into my office at Fangsters, Harvey shook his head at me. Because of our connection he experienced every second of my humiliating experience.

"Oh, be quiet," I said. "It wasn't a total loss."

"Mm hmm."

"The Fang Hunter isn't a local mage. I'm certain of that now. I can cross the number one suspect off René's suspect hit list."

"Mm." Harvey nodded slowly.

"I know. I know. I should be careful with my magic levels, but I had to show those twittering mages my power."

"I saw that. Pink fog that smells like cotton candy. Yup. You sure showed them."

I firmed my lips and counted to ten, as I took a pain killer out of my office drawer.

"Darlin', I don't mean to fault you."

But he so did! I exhaled slowly, a feeble attempt to temper the rage that swirled inside me like a cyclone. I downed the prescribed pills.

"But" he continued, "you need to look at yourself in the mirror. That show-off blast fried you."

I put a hand to my hair. Oh, hell in a cauldron. My hair felt crispy. That wasn't a good sign. My shoulders ached with tension. My eyes stung. And true to form, a nasty migraine brewed in the top of my head. I groaned. "Maybe," I said.

"You better lie down before you collapse on the floor."

Again, the darn rabbit made a good point. I crawled onto the sofa beneath the window and managed to pull the blanket over me before I fell into a deep sleep.

Powerful witches totally control their dreams. Even the average witch next door can exert some will over her night adventures. But not me. Never. Ever. I careened into bedlam.

I FOUND myself in my bedroom at the academy, reliving the last time I saw Onyx. Why? I asked my subconscious. Why? Why do I have to do this twice when I didn't like it the first time? But my subconscious didn't answer. She's like that.

Onyx, looking as handsome as ever, stood a foot from me. The golden specks in his obsidian eyes blazed with anger. His predator presence would make any sane mortal shiver even without his rage, but I was far beyond reacting that way to him regardless of his mood. As far as I was concerned, he was a bad houseguest who'd outstayed his visit.

"Just tell your family." His voice sounded deep and gravelly.

"I can't." The knot I held so firmly in my stomach twisted. "I can't. Don't you understand how blackmail works? Alessandro controls me. My secret cannot be revealed. Not now. Not ever. And he knows it."

Onyx let my words hang. The air around us smelled deliciously male. Why couldn't I have an ugly night stalker for Fangster's head of security, instead of a hot one with deadly charm, enough sex appeal to melt a glacier, and a razor-sharp mind ... who had begun to care for me?

He had dark-chocolate-brown eyes that drew me in with a mere glance, a square chin covered with just the right amount of scruff to make my female parts whimper, and chiseled cheekbones a runway model would die for. And that was just his face. He also had broad shoulders, a thin waist, and long legs. The guy belonged on the cover of a romance novel.

While Onyx was a man most would drool over, his good looks and vampiric charm didn't work so well on me at first. His personality drove me crazy. Even if I learned to ignore his biting sarcasm, horrible taste in music, and peculiar habits he picked up from living in the shadows, I had to work and live with him under the same roof, twenty-four-seven. So, I didn't like-like him.

And yet ... and yet, Onyx cared enough to ask me about my problem. That meant something, didn't it? I thought he disliked me as much as I did him, but maybe, just maybe, we could be a couple.

Onyx inhaled a sharp breath and spoke in the same exasperated, dismissive voice he used on our students when they didn't get what he was saying. "This is what I know. A blackmailer controls you only as long as you have a secret. If you reveal it, he loses his power over you. So, the solution is simple. Kick your damn skeleton out of the closet."

"I. Can't."

His eyes softened.

My knees wobbled.

He shook his head. "Think about it. Right now, you hold the power to control how your secret is revealed. You can determine who you tell, and how much you reveal. If you take charge of the situation, you can manage how much damage will be done."

"No. Just, no! You don't understand. If my secret is revealed, my whole life will be ruined."

He shook his head. "You're impossible."

"You don't know my secret."

His mouth hitched on one side. "I know this ... What matters most to you is your family. The secret must involve them. I also know they all love you, unconditionally. They will get over whatever transgression you've made." He tucked a lock of my hair behind my ear.

My breath hitched at his touch, and my lips trembled. "You just don't understand."

"Then tell me. Make me understand. This control Alessandro has over you is not healthy."

I blinked back a tear. "Being controlled by a powerful vampire is not something I planned on. I hate it. But ... the academy is ..." I hesitated, wanting to say good, or maybe professionally challenging, or at least okay, but instead I said, "Interesting."

Onyx scoffed. "You can't tell me you would choose to work here."

"Well ..."

"Or choose to be awoken and given orders in the middle

of the night by one of the deadliest vampires in all the realms."

He had me there. Alessandro's night visits made my skin crawl. "Look, Onyx, I'm enjoying our truce." Though the word enjoying fell short of addressing the emotional fireworks that sparked between the two of us—or the soul-searing heat neither of us admitted to feeling. "And I respect your advice." Some of the time. "But I cannot tell the world my secret. Ever!"

"Then Alessandro will command you, forever. It's your choice."

"No!" I screamed because I couldn't let that happen. But I also couldn't tell Onyx that I had a plan to deal with Alessandro in a witch way. "No," I said more calmly. "Once I have the school running smoothly, I am confident he will let me move on."

Onyx's brows rose. "And I thought you were—" His body froze with his words hanging in the air.

Previously I remembered him saying, "Smart," but in this dream, he did not. In this dream, he stopped and stared at me with wonder. As if ... As if ...

"Onyx, what do you want to tell me?"

His body reanimated. "Help," he said. "I need help." His image disappeared.

"Onyx!" I screamed.

I WOKE myself up with the scream, gasping for breath. My hands felt clammy, and my throat felt drier than the Sahara Desert.

"Interesting," said Harvey as he hopped onto the sofa to

sit beside me. "Onyx used a dream to communicate with you."

"He did."

"The dhamphyre is more powerful than I thought."

I closed my eyes for a moment, refusing to give Onyx a compliment. "He utilized an emotional moment to communicate with me because my senses would be most awake during that time. A strategic move. A smart move. Very Onyx."

Harvey's cheeks puffed in and out. "Mm hmm."

I swiped at the tears on my cheeks. "Onyx is captive, and I have no idea where."

"At least you know he's alive," murmured Harvey.

"But in trouble." I pulled the blanket closer around my body. "It's not like Onyx to ask me for help. He would only do that if his life was in danger, and he had no other choice."

CHAPTER NINE

Tick Tock – 25 hours left.

As soon as the sun slid below the coastal mountains, I met with Gavin and René in my office. I motioned for them to take a seat across my desk.

Gavin wore a perfectly pressed police uniform topped with a cop scowl. He nodded and folded his muscular body into a chair.

René, my savant vampire student sank onto the other chair with the grace of an aristocrat at a prestigious gentleman's club. He appeared to be seventeen, but in real time he was my age, twenty-five, and cut a dashingly handsome figure. His young face dominated by big, brown eyes were outlined by the longest, curly eyelashes I had ever seen. His dark skin had a healthy glow, and he smelled like the crisp night air.

"I'll cut to the chase," I said. "The Fang Hunter has Onyx."

Gavin grunted. "Figured that."

René cleared his throat. "I've organized all the vampires

in town. As we speak, search parties scour the grounds for clues. Try not to worry, Ms. Rebel. We will find him."

Says a dead man. I scoffed. "Thank you for that and thank you for leaving us a report." I fingered the file on my desk. "I infiltrated the mage guild today, and long story short—we can rule them out. That leaves Claudia and the stranger."

Gavin's denim-blue eyes darkened almost to black like a perfect storm brewing on the horizon. "You didn't stick to the plan."

"No, I didn't."

He growled so loud the vibration made my teaching license on the wall shake. "My pack is roaming the forest trails. Donovan has the shifters covering the mountain and wizards scrying." He stopped for a moment and looked toward the window. "The local cops are managing all the checkpoints we've set up." His nostrils flared. "And the town witches, well, they're doing what witches do."

I made a face at him, knowing he had said that just to annoy me.

René lifted his chin. "When I left the residences, I asked Ice to bring Claudia to us in ten minutes. They should be here any second now. She's number two on my list."

Teachers aren't supposed to have favorites, but if I did, Ice would be one of them. He was a muscle-bound guy of few words. But he had a big heart. His impulsiveness unfortunately got him into a lot of trouble, and that's how he ended up at Fangsters under my supervision. But his heart was helping him find his way.

Gavin turned to René. "You do the questioning. I'll observe." Then he glanced my way.

"Okay," I said.

Ice, wearing his trademark gray sweat suit with the

word Fangsters across the chest, escorted the young woman in. He nodded to me.

According to her student file, Claudia was a two-hundred-year-old vampire who Alessandro turned at the age of eighteen to save her from dying from syphilis. While she had behaved for the first century and a half of her undead life, she had recently got into a lot of trouble.

A few weeks ago, Alessandro had found her feeding on people without their permission in a homeless encampment, telling them the blood-letting would improve their health. She had been at Fangsters for two weeks, and I had had little interaction with her—on account of always being snowed under paperwork.

I took a moment to study Claudia. Her chubby cheeks had a youthful glow, and her crystal-blue eyes dared me to speak to her. Overall, she didn't give a menacing vibe. To look at her, you would never guess that she had ever done anything worse than eat too much cake, which puzzled me. Being plump was rare for a vampire. Didn't their high metabolism keep them thin? Maybe it was optional. I'd have to ask Onyx about that.

Onyx. I swallowed.

Since the last time I saw her, she had dyed her short hair black. It had been a lovely shade of pink, and I had no freaking idea what her natural color was, but then again, I'm not sure dead people have a natural color. Anyway, she had gelled her hair to stand on end, and wore a leather dog collar. I sniffed, to let her know I could smell drugs on her and gave her a prim all-business smile.

She sneered at Ice, "You're just a gopher on 'roids. Go find yourself someone else to rat out."

Ice snarled at her and then looked at me. "I'll stand outside the door. Call me, if you need me, Ms. Rebel."

"Thank you, Ice."

As the door closed behind him, I motioned to Claudia to sit in the empty chair Gavin had vacated. He stood by the window.

René turned his full attention to Claudia. "Do you know why you're here?"

"Let me guess—someone complained about me. Someone is always complaining about me." She grumbled. "The residences are crammed AF. There's no bloody privacy in this place. It's like a prison."

Not for the first time, I wished I could see the vampire's lair. Leaning forward, I got right in her face. "Why were you not in your coffin at sunset ... the last two evenings?"

She narrowed her eyes. "Hah." She leaned back. "Is that what this is about?"

"Yes. There's a Fang Hunter on the loose, and we need to account for where everyone slept the night, he attacked Xiu."

"Yeah, yeah, I heard about him, the guy who woke up short a fang." She huffed. "Well, it wasn't me. You can't possibly think it was me." She shriveled up her nose and turned to René. "*C'est moi?*"

"Where were you?" he asked in a lighter voice, as if he were just making conversation. Given his soft French accent, I would have told him anything, but Claudia just shrugged in a cold mind-your-effen-business way.

After a couple beats, she huffed and confessed. "Okay, I'll tell you. I lay with Harrison."

René arched a trimmed brow. "And if I asked her, she would confirm this?"

"I don't see why not. There's no law against co-casketing is there?" She glanced at me and back at René.

"Don't tell me there's a stupid Fangster rule about where we rest."

I felt totally beyond my depth. Co-casketing? I'd never heard of such a thing. Gavin hadn't moved a muscle.

René firmed his jaw. "No, of course not. It's just not something ..."

"That you do?" Claudia laughed. "A little too intimate?"

"Um," he muttered.

"Listen, sonny, when you've been dead for more than a century, you'll understand." She looked at me. "The loneliness gets to you, and it's nice to fall into the deathly state, in the arms of another."

"But the smell!" said René. Sweat popped on his forehead.

"Intimate. You obviously missed the word, René. It is something one does with a lover." She sighed. "It's been decades since I lay with Harrison, but it felt right."

"So," I said, trying to move the discussion back to more pressing matters than dead bodies wrapped in each other's arms. "You have no idea who the Fang Hunter is."

"None." Her face drew long. "But if I catch him, he or she will be missing more than their teeth."

René cleared his throat. "I'll talk with Harrison."

Claudia shrugged and looked at her perfectly polished black fingernails.

Gavin walked over, "Was anyone missing this morning?"

"No," René responded. "All fangsters are accounted for but ... we have one more missing fang."

I cringed. "Who?"

"Joy Graves, the oldest vampire student. We've sedated her, because she went ballistic. I hope to be able to question her soon."

I swallowed. "We've ruled out the mages and Claudia. That leaves us with the theory that the Fang Hunter is a stranger. And I have no idea where to start looking for them."

"What about the staff?" Claudia asked. "They're as creepy as they come if you ask me."

CHAPTER TEN

Tick Tock – 6 hours left.

While René and Gavin oversaw the search teams for the Fang Hunter, I spent hours going through the student and staff personnel files thinking that maybe I had missed something. But I came up with nothing. Yeah, the vampire students had all exhibited less than appropriate behavior during their undead lives, but they did nothing that was unexpected for night stalkers. There were no signs that any of them would be involved in selling vampire body parts on the black market. It would not only be a morally reprehensible thing for them to do; it would also be plain stupid. Few dared to challenge the number one law of the vampire code—thou shalt not harm another vampire for financial gain.

Just the thought of doing so made me wince. Not because of what the law states, but because of all it doesn't state. Clearly, vampires considered it fine to harm another vampire for jealousy, or entertainment, but you couldn't do it if a price tag was involved. I shook my head. Would I ever understand vampire culture? If Onyx was here, he would argue that the undead had come to this decision through living immortal lives that spanned centuries, and therefore it held a wisdom beyond my small mortal brain's comprehension. I shivered. Even in his absence, the shadow man got under my skin.

Harvey put his paw on my hand. "So, the files on your staff reveal little of interest. What's your next step, darlin'?"

"More research," I groaned and flicked on an Internet search window.

Within the hour my eyes burned from spending too much time on the screen, and as I studied the fang trade my headache came back to haunt me.

"But what did you learn?" asked Harvey who had snoozed while I worked.

"The one fact that repeatedly jumps out me is that while lots of fangs are traded in the nine realms, vampire fangs are most prized. The bottom price for one fang is a million dollars, and the amount goes up depending on the incisor's age and heritage."

I leaned back into my chair as the pre-dawn light glowed on the horizon heralding the start of another summer day.

"What now?" nagged Harvey.

"I'll make a new to-do list." I bit my lip. "This time I'll focus on the academy."

To-Do List

1. *Plunge my head into a bowl of ice-cold water and scream.*
2. *Nail the Fang Hunter.*
3. *Find Onyx.*

~

I HESITATED ON NUMBER THREE. Trained teams of supernatural beings and norm cops were out looking for Onyx and the Fang Hunter. What could I do, that they couldn't? I tapped my pen on my desk for a minute, and then it dawned on me. The answer was simple.

"Darlin', I don't like the look on your face," said Harvey, sitting up straight in his chair.

"I'm going to search the residences." The vampires won't let the cops down there. While the bloodsuckers did their own investigation of the crime scene. I had no way of knowing how thorough they were being. Besides, I might see something they didn't. "I could use my witch senses."

Harvey thumped his paw on his forehead. "Alessandro forbade you to go down there. He said in no uncertain words to not ... go ... there." The rabbit sniffed. "I think he added, ever."

"I have no choice."

"He said never. Ever. Darlin'."

"I have ... no ... choice."

"It's dangerous, my witch."

Harvey only called me '*my witch*,' when he was truly worried, but I waved his words away with my hand. "I have to be ready to take on whatever lies below ground." In the bowels of my academy. I shivered. The security of Fangsters relied on me.

“It can’t be worse than what’s above ground,” I said out loud.

“Oh … but it can,” said Harvey jumping up to stand on his paws. “No one invades a vampire’s lair and lives to talk about it.” His eyes widened. “Don’t do it.”

CHAPTER ELEVEN

Tick Tock 4 hours left ... Doom looms.

Convinced that all the answers to the mystery lay below ground, I strode toward the basement door. The entranceway was situated underneath the grand staircase, as if it were the door to Harry Potter's room.

Harvey followed me, grumbling all the way. "You won't listen to me. You won't listen to reason. You won't even listen to the big, bad vampire. Have you no sense, *my witch*?"

A black metal sign hung above the door, *All Mortals Beware – Forbidden Area.* The words had been painted in a blood red color. I swallowed my fear as a chill ran up my spine. I had no choice.

I knew when I opened the access point, I would find a wooden staircase that led to the basement of the manor, which housed the student, faculty, and guest residences. I had glimpsed it many times.

I also knew the so-called crypt was connected to a

network of tunnels that lay below the town. Originally built by smugglers over a hundred years ago, they snaked from caves on the shoreline to the downtown area and beyond.

Alessandro had built his own lair down there somewhere and appropriated the rest of the space for his kind, a fact that rankled other supernaturals in town. Vampire patrols kept them private and secure. I had no idea what the maze looked like. In the beginning of my tenure at the academy, Alessandro promised me a tour in the future, but that future never came. My brothers had wanted access, but they too had been denied.

I huffed as I reread the sign. "How am I supposed to protect my students, when I'm not allowed inside their residences—the very place where they're being attacked?"

"That, my darlin', is a good question, but beside the point. You need to stay out and stay safe."

I pretended not to hear Harvey. "My night stalkers are vulnerable when they sleep. It's my job to protect them."

I felt the rabbit roll his eyes. "Darlin', the undead don't exactly sleep. You know that, right?"

I stopped and squinted at him. "Well, that's the thing, I'm not sure what they do in their down time."

"They play—dead." Harvey sucked in his cheeks, and his nose turned bright pink.

"Dead. It sounds so final for such lively beings."

Harvey arched a hairy brow. "You've been hanging out with bloodsuckers far too long."

"Mm. To hex with it, I'm going down." I took another step toward the door. I was close enough to touch it now.

"Into their lair?" Harvey's whiskers spun faster than a ceiling fan on high speed.

"Yes."

"Think about it, Rebel. Don't you want their permission?"

"Onyx isn't here to protect the students. My predator friends are all out cold. Dead. Whatever. That leaves me. I must do something." Tears of frustration welled in my eyes. "Sitting in my office isn't helping anyone. I must do this. I have to save their fangs."

"I'll be right behind you," Harvey said. But he sure didn't sound happy about it.

"Mm." I considered my situation. I have a heroic, invisible bunny for back up, and I'm about to face an evil Fang Hunter in the den of delinquent vampires who have made it abundantly clear on many, many occasions, that I should not trespass into their space. Could my crazy life get any crazier?

"I really wish you didn't keep asking that question," mumbled Harvey.

"Stay here," I told him.

As I grabbed the doorknob, I called on my magic, and all the gods and goddesses of the universe. It wasn't a time to play favorites. I wanted all the energy—of all that is—on my side. It was, after all, the righteous side. Right?

"Isn't that what all soldiers say when they enter battle?" Harvey mumbled. "You really aren't good at this."

"Shut it."

As I turned the door handle, it felt preternaturally cold. With the help of a silent opening spell, I rotated it, the door hinges creaked, and the simple wooden portal opened wide.

The smell of damp earth, sweaty socks, and death hit me between my eyes like a butcher's mallet. It was not a welcoming experience, but at least I knew I was in the right place. I raised my chin, ready to enter the vampire's crypt.

The wooden staircase led to an old stone staircase that descended further down into the earth. I couldn't see the end of it in the inky darkness.

"I ... I ... don't like this," said Harvey who saw everything through my mind.

"I can handle it." I stilled my senses. "Stay above ground, Harvey. No matter what happens. Stay above ground."

Of course, there were no lights in this passageway. I should have expected that. Vampires can see in the dark, so they don't need electric bulbs. I pulled out my phone and turned on the flashlight. Slowly, step by step, I descended into the bowels of my academy. My stomach clenching tighter every second.

The stench of death grew stronger the further I ventured. At the end of the stairway, I found a solid metal door with locks. Trust Onyx to secure the residences with the latest technology. It looked like something in a James Bond movie.

I cast a beam of laser light from my fingers to release the locks. The door opened silently. I think I would have felt better if it creaked. The stillness of the silence sent a shiver up my spine. I peered inside, illuminating the area with my flashlight. It appeared to be a large room, about the size of the library upstairs, with ten-foot earthen walls strengthened by wooden beams.

Gingerly, I stepped inside. The basement was darker than night and stiller than death. My heart leaped into my throat. I didn't belong here and that feeling echoed in my bones. I struggled for my next breath.

The smell of dead bodies grew stronger. My stomach flipped, and I wanted to run. In my head Harvey said, *I told you so.*

I had to think. How else would Onyx protect the vampire nest? Would daggers fly out of the wall like in a treasure hunting movie? Or maybe worse, bats? I hate bats.

I swallowed and took another step. Nothing moved. I was just being silly, scaring myself, as if I was a thirteen-year-old at a Halloween sleepover. Nothing was going to—

Clang. Scrape. Clang. Scrape.

I froze. The sounds came from the other end of the room, the darkest area. What or who had I awakened? I turned off my light and listened.

The clanking drew nearer. I crouched beside the door ready to flee—or attack. My heart pounded like a jackhammer. Goosebumps rose on my arms.

Clang. Scrape. Clang. Scrape. Whoever it was—whatever it was—crept steadily toward me. My nose wiggled. I smelled a chemical, possibly chloroform. If only I could turn on my light. But that would be stupid.

Screech. The squeal of old hinges turning cut into the night. I studied the shadows in the darkness. A dark figure opened the top of a coffin. My fingers itched to send a message on my phone to Gavin, but I couldn't risk making any noise or movement. I had to deal with this on my own.

A rustling followed. Rustling? I had no idea what that could be. *Pop.* That sound I knew from visits to the dentist. A tooth—a fang—had been pulled.

My body shook and my hands trembled violently.

"Hmm. Gotcha, bloodsucker," said a male voice with glee.

Anger roiled inside me. I wish I could say it was courage, but it was more like pure hot rage, and it made me move. I shone my flashlight toward the source of the voice.

There, three yards in front of me, stood Norm the academy's norm janitor. He leaned over the open casket. In one hand he held a pair of pliers, and in the other a cloth soaked in something with a strong chemical smell wrapped around a fang.

"How could you?" I screamed loud enough to wake the dead.

His rheumy eyes glinted with pure malice. "Oh, it's you, the goody-goody witch."

"These are my students. *Our* students. I can't let you hurt them."

He scoffed. "They're creatures of the night. Blood-sucking killers, every one of them. Vampires don't belong in our town. You must know that in your soul." He hissed and spit flew from his mouth. "If you have a soul. None of you magic folk belong in my town."

"Put your pliers down," I ordered.

A muscle twitched in his cheek. "Okay, if you don't care about vampires living amongst us, listen to this. I make more than a million cold bucks on every tooth I harvest. I'll give you a percentage to keep your mouth shut." The line between his eyes deepened. "If you help me, we can harvest two fangs tonight, and you'll have more money that you could ever make being a teacher."

"These vampires are under my protection."

"What are you going to do about it? Throw a high heel at my head."

Well ... Well, he should be afraid of me. I paused. He should be very afraid of me. I was a witch after all, and he was a norm with no powers. So, why the hex wasn't he afraid. What ...?

"Urrgh." A deep voice from behind me made a gruesome noise, rattling my senses.

I turned.

There stood a ten-foot demon. Sometimes, I don't like it when the universe answers my questions.

CHAPTER
TWELVE

I gazed up at the blazing red eyes of the beast and tried not to flinch. It's never wise to flinch in the face of a demon. But of course I did and he licked his lips.

"You called in the devil's squad?" I said to Norm.

He chuckled. "It's part of my business plan. Selling a piece of my soul for demonic backup is worth the cost," he hissed.

"Norm, you're an idiot. There is no such thing as selling *a piece* of your soul. There are no subdivisions on divine light. Once the devil gets a foothold, he takes it all. And you have no way to get it back."

"I don't care. I'm buying a yacht and I will sail the seven seas."

Of course, he didn't care. I exhaled slowly. My less than admirable witch powers could not take on a demon. I could hope that some latent fae magic might kick in, but that was like making a wish upon a star in a galaxy far, far away. I had to think fast.

The beast gurgled. There are many kinds of demons, the gurgling ones were never my favorite. They had small brains and obeyed their masters without hesitation. They also considered witches a treat to eat. I've been told we taste like caramel pudding. Reasoning with this guy was out of the question. My only option was to reason with the janitor.

"Norm, stop this nonsense. Now. You can't get away with killing me. My family will hunt you down."

"Hmph. I took Onyx with no trouble. I can handle the rest." A wicked smile spread across his craggy face.

My mouth dropped. He had nabbed Onyx! I swallowed. Norm was right, I wasn't more powerful than the dhamphre. The bitter taste of defeat filled my mouth. And the quiet of the dead vampires' lair chilled me to the bone. This couldn't be happening. We were all going to be victims of one greedy, norm. I swallowed. I closed my searching for a solution.

"Wait, what did you do with Onyx?"

"Nothing yet. You like him, don't you?"

"Like? No. He's, my assistant."

"Mm hmm. I've seen how you two look at each other, like lions without food. It's quite nauseating for the rest of us, you know."

I did not. He did not. *We* did not look like hungry lions. "So, you're holding Onyx somewhere nearby?"

Norm lifted his chin in a regal way. "I told my demon to imprison him in one of the caverns in the tunnels. Before you start thinking you can play hero, let me tell you, Onyx cannot be freed. Even if you find him, and you won't, he can't escape the demonic spell cast upon him."

A demonic spell! "What are you up to?"

Norm's chest puffed out. "Onyx is a rare supernatural specimen—a dhamphre. He's worth cold cash. I've set up an auction on the dark web. So far, the highest bid is three million in untraceable diamonds. I know if I released his name, I could get more, but I don't want that kind of attention. I'm a shrewd businessman." The wicked smile returned. "I'll give the bidding a week and then take the highest amount."

"That's so ... cold," I said. "Selling another person, that's even worse than selling a fang."

"It's my escape money, honey." His eyes had never looked so calculating. Who knew the janitor with fun stories had such schemes growing inside of him?

"Well," I said. "You do seem to have thought of everything."

"*Gurgle*."

A chill crawled up my spine as the demon mumbled something unintelligible.

Norm scratched his paunch. "I suppose I could auction you off as well. But I'm not sure who would be interested in a scrawny book nerd of a witch. Hmm ... What can you offer me in return for saving your life?"

Revulsion flooded my senses, twisting the knot in my stomach tighter. Surely, he wasn't suggesting what I thought he was suggesting. "What do you want from me?"

Spirrr. Whiz. Sprirr. Whiz. The sound of small drones buzzed in the stale air as they moved towards Norm.

He whirled around to face them.

Meanwhile, the demon's heavy hand landed on my shoulder. I stepped hard on his foot.

"*Urgh*." The demon's body jolted, but he didn't move.

I twisted beneath his hand, and his grip tightened. The beast smelled worse than a vat of rotting fish.

"No," screamed Norm to the drones. "No!" He threw up his hands to protect himself from their attack. The three drones orbited him, making clicking noises.

"Go aw—"

Norm's words stopped as a long blade protruded from one of the drones and sliced his head off in one smooth swoop. It fell to the ground and bounced, leaving his convulsing body to crumple.

Horror and shock froze me for a moment. I watched as one of the killer drones circled Norm's body and snapped photos. The other two drones moved towards the demon and me.

I gulped. The demon gurgled.

The drones circled us three times communicating with each other through more clicking sounds.

The demon's eyes blazed with hellfire, and his gurgles deepened, but the machines didn't care. As they became within reach, the demon pushed me away from him and swatted at them with his massive, clawed hands.

The robots predicted his movements and ducked out of his reach.

I stood still watching in horror as the monster fought for his life. What else could I do?

Would I be next? If this was to be the end, I wanted to go on my terms—at peace with myself. A single tear trickled down my cheek. I swiped it away with the back of my hand. This was no time for self-pity. I had to face death, as I had life—head on. I took a deep breath and waited for the end.

Death by drones. I had never imagined that!

The demon didn't give up. He kept swatting at the machines. The killer drone released its blade readying for attack. As the demon reached out to grab it, another appeared with a blade and sliced his hand off.

The demon howled loud enough to raise hell itself. Frantically he reached with his other hand to grab the other drone, but it moved out of the way at the last second.

The sour stench of demon blood burned my nose, as one drone moved closer to him.

But I couldn't worry about the monster, as the two other drones sped towards me. They circled my shaking body three times, beeping like manic microwave ovens out of control. It was a different sound from their clicking.

I was sure my time had come, but, as suddenly as the assassin drones arrived, they turned returned into the darkness of the back tunnels. It all happened in less than five minutes, and yet it felt like an eternity. The knot in my stomach that I thought could not get tighter, tightened.

Norm, the Fang Hunter was lay dead in a puddle of his own blood. His pet demon was left without a master, roaring in pain, but still alive. I let out a long slow breath. Would the drones return? I scanned the darkness and listened, but there was no sign of them.

What the hex had just happened? Why was I spared? Maybe the drones had been programmed to identify me and not kill me. I know René built drones for a hobby. Maybe they were his creations. I shook my head. If a cat has nine lives, I must have a hundred.

The monster gurgled as looked down at me. My fight for survival wasn't over. I closed my eyes for a second to gather my strength. It was far from over. I tried to swallow my fear but couldn't as I knew I had to face the demonic beast bellowing in pain from his many wounds. I opened my eyes. Green blood oozed from large gashes in his body. He lurched towards me.

We locked gazes assessing one another.

His eyes blazed with hellfire. I called on my magic and screamed, "No!"

He raised his hand to reach for me.

I tilted my head. Could he understand me?

He stepped closer.

"No one steps into my space," I said in my sorceress voice. Plasma bolts flew out of my fingers and hit him in his chest.

He jumped back and yowled so loud the hair on the nape of my neck stood on end. His eyes blazed even brighter.

I zapped him again. This time in his eyes.

He screamed in agony and staggered back, holding his face in his hands.

My body trembled from the exertion. The two acts of magic had totally depleted my energy. I had nothing left. "Go back to where you came from," I growled.

The beast lunged at me. I had just enough time to raise my fae pendant to my heart, a desperate last move, that came to me instinctively. Much to my surprise it flashed a beacon of bright green light that zapped the demon in the neck. He dematerialized on the spot, leaving a pile of gray ash on the cement floor.

I gasped. The beast was gone! My pendant felt warm in my hand. What made me grab it at the last instant? I had no idea the talisman left to me by my fae grandmother had that kind of power. I considered it a sentimental gift, a link to that side of my family. I never expected it to save my life. I held it to my heart once more. "Thank you, Grandma Queen Erynn of the Fae high court."

But there was no time to digest the scene. There may never be enough time to comprehend everything that had just happened. I had to move on.

Onyx was being held by a demonic spell. He needed me. I stared at the dead body of Norm, the Fang Hunter and shivered. He lay motionless on the ground, in a puddle of his own blood flowing from his neck. I held my nose as I searched his pockets for keys. As soon as I found them, I ran as fast as I could to the tunnel entrance behind him.

With Norm dead, I wasn't sure how long the demon's master, for surely, he had a master, would bother keeping Onyx alive. I had to get to rescue him.

CHAPTER THIRTEEN

Was I too late? What if he's dead? What if I have to manage the academy without him? What if I have to live ... without him?

As I entered the tunnels all I could think about was time. It disappeared too bloody fast. There were so many things I wanted to say to Onyx ... needed to say ... and may never get to say. He might die without knowing my true feelings. Onyx may be the most infuriating night stalker in all the realms, but ... I wanted him to live.

The tunnel entrance was large enough for a subway car to enter, but it narrowed quickly. The walls changed from concrete to earth. The stale air smelled of rat dung, vampires, and something sinister that I couldn't quite put my finger on. I moved as fast as I could, not knowing where or how to find Onyx, not knowing if more drones, or some other deadly device, would leap out at me at any moment like in an Indiana Jones movie; not knowing how I could free Onyx when I found him. All I knew was that I had to find him.

The tunnel—now just large enough for me to stand in

—meandered like a bad nightmare. Water dripped down the earthen walls, and rats scuttled along the ground. In the distance, I could hear a fan whirling.

The underpass took a sharp turn to the north, and I came to a stop facing a junction of three new tunnels. While they all tracked north, they did so at different angles.

The first one, to my right, was the narrowest. It reminded me of burrows criminals dig under international borders. The walls had been scraped away roughly, possibly by hand. It could collapse easily at any moment and it smelled gross. I didn't want to think of what had been stashed inside that space.

The middle shaft, directly in front me, had a line of unlit torches. Though wider it too had earthen walls. No doubt it had been left behind by the smugglers.

The third one, the one on my left, surprised me. It had cement block walls and fresher air. The sound of the fan came from somewhere inside it.

While I would prefer to traverse the more finished tunnel, I had to decide which one a demon would use to hide Onyx? Panting, I wiped sweat from my face and forced myself to concentrate.

If I were a demon I would choose the most remote location, the one the vampires would be least likely to explore. I reached out with my witch senses and tried to locate Onyx one more time.

It took a couple minutes, but I detected faint breathing down the first tunnel. Of course, it would be the most dangerous, the smelliest, and by far the creepiest tunnel. I swallowed hard and walked into the tiny underpass the one that reeked like a freshly dug grave.

Inside, the stench of death grew stronger. Was this where vampires hid corpses? They weren't supposed to kill people, but I could smell rotting flesh. I gagged and pushed on.

One hundred yards in, I stumbled on a rock and fell face first onto the mucky dirt floor. In the process, my mouth filled with mud. Ugh. It tasted as bad as it smelled. I spit it out. Was there flesh in it?

Pushing myself up on to my knees, I vowed, "If I ever get out of this Goddess forsaken hellhole, I'll take charge of my life. No more drifting in the currents of other people's lives. No more bowing to vampires."

On all fours, I could see a small hole in the wall. If I had continued walking, I probably wouldn't have seen it, as it lay a foot above my current eye level.

Could I make myself squeeze into that small a space? I crawled through the muck and into the dark opening. As I moved, the sound of someone breathing became louder. The entranceway narrowed until the sides pressed against my body, and the ceiling against my back. I pulled my body along the ground as the space narrowed even more. The demon must have used another entrance. Why couldn't I find that one.

The breathing sound became clearer. It was faint and raspy as if the person didn't have much time left. Desperately I pulled myself through the filth and slime. With every pull, the sound of the slow inhale and exhale grew louder. I kept pulling until the tunnel opened into a rock cavern.

I squeezed myself out of the hole and landed on my feet on a rock surface. I was in one of the many caves that dot our shoreline. I inhaled the clean, salty air, and looked around the space with my flashlight.

There was Onyx!

His still body lay on a sandstone boulder to the right

side of the cave. Thick ropes held him still. on top. His face looked gray as if his life was draining away.

My pulse quickened as I watched his chest rise and fall. He was alive. Well, as alive as an undead hybrid relic of the netherworld could be. I looked around. We were alone. Relief gushed into me with the force of a tsunami. I felt lighthearted, jubilant, ecstatic, and ran to his side.

"Onyx. Onyx. Wake up."

No response.

I shook his arm. Nothing. What had the demon's magic done to him? A sigil marked his forehead; two interlocking ovals contained within a circle. It glowed an eerie shade of green. It had to be the signature of a powerful demon. Did the sigil hold the power to keep Onyx in a coma?

I scanned the area for a potion bottle, hex bag, or anything else that could explain his condition. But all I kept coming back to the sigil.

I could hear ocean waves hitting the rocks below and the clicking sound of bats. I shivered. How I hate bats. I tried my phone, but the signal wasn't strong enough. It kept crapping out just before it made a connection. I could try a telepathic link with my sisters, but I was never good at that kind of magic, and I had little energy left.

There was just me and Onyx, alone, and in trouble.

"*Caw. Caw. Caw.*" I froze at the familiar sound of the raven's call.

He flew through the open space and alighted on Onyx's chest.

"Not now. Shoo," I said to it. "Go away. I'll find you some crumbs later."

His eerie midnight-blue eyes glared at me for a second, and then he dove at my neck and pecked it.

"Owe!" I cursed him and pressing my palm over my bleeding neck.

As I readied my magic to blast the raven, he flew back onto the top of Onyx's chest.

"Go away," I yelled. Hadn't Harvey said something about Ravens eating corpses.

The midnight black raven lifted his beak soaked in my blood to the ceiling of the cave and dissolved—or so it appeared. He was there one moment, and the next he was not. The bird of prey simply melted into Onyx.

What the hex?

Onyx stirred as the sigil on his forehead vanished. "Mm."

"Onyx, wake up." I shook his arm.

Slowly he opened his eyes and stared at me. Relief flooded my system.

"It took you long enough," he said.

CHAPTER

FOURTEEN

I expected an explanation for the raven transformation but got none.

Bursting through the ropes that held him in place, Onyx rose to a sitting position. "You don't belong down here," he barked.

"But—"

He pressed a finger to his mouth. "Not here. It's not safe for you."

"But?"

He shook his head and pointed toward the tunnel that led back to the academy. "Go. Now. Back the way you came. Go ... while you still can."

The way he spoke filled me with terror. Seriously. If he, the mighty predator, was scared for me, I ought to be scared too. So, I hustled, back through the muck and more muck and more muck, not to mentions stench; back to the tunnel where I could stand again. Then I ran as fast as I could.

I passed Norm's dead body and passed the demon's ashes. I was almost out of the vampire's crypt when I came to a dead stop. The stillness of the night stalker's nest was deafening but also alluring. I had to do a double take of the situation. I might never get another opportunity to witness the undead in their slumber state. I pulled out my phone and snapped a few pictures. What would a couple minutes cost me?

Energy was the answer. As I climbed the stairs back to the main floor, exhaustion and adrenalin withdrawal hit me hard. Or maybe it was shock. I don't know. My body trembled, my head ached, and my muscles refused to function properly. I slowed down but kept going.

That's when I heard something approaching me from behind.

Not again. More drones? I tried to quicken my pace, but my body felt heavier than cement. I was so tired. So very tired. All I wanted to do was collapse. Maybe this was as good an end for me as any.

Flap. Flap. Flap. Skuttle. Skuttle. I spun around to face the sounds and squinted into the dark. A horde of bats shot toward me. "Bats!" I screeched feeling terror flow through my veins as if it were my life blood. It would have to be bats. But they weren't alone. A sea of hairy spiders skittled along the walls.

I screamed.

Two enormous hands grabbed me by the waist. I looked up and faced Alessandro my nemesis. He threw me over his shoulder and carried me the rest of the way up the stairs. Carefully he lowered my mud-soaked body onto the sofa in the front foyer of the main floor of the academy.

Tears streamed down my face. I shook with fear, shock, and pure terror, but that didn't stop me from punching him in the stomach as hard as I could. "Owe!" I felt like I hit steel.

He didn't flinch, but he did grunt.

"Onyx is alive," I said.

"I know. He contacted me to save you."

"You know?" It took a second for that thought to settle in to my riddled mind. "I caught the Fang Hunter," I added.

He firmed his square jaw and nodded his approval. "I saw his body parts."

I closed my eyes. It was over.

"Rebel." Alessandro cupped my chin and lifted it, forcing me to look at him. "Never, ever go into the tunnels again."

"Got any other how-to survival tips?"

He chuckled in that manly way of his that irritates the hell out of me, but then everything about the blood-sucking blackmailer bugged me. He vanished without a goodbye. Not even a 'good job' comment. Nope. Nothing. Once again, I had met his demands within his timeline and for now, my secret was safe.

Harvey appeared at my side. As I wiped tears from my face I said to him, "Just another crazy day living in the house of the rising dead."

CHAPTER
FIFTEEN

The next morning René delivered a big bouquet of black roses, a box of pistachio macrons (my favorite) and a note: *On behalf of all the vampires in our academy, we thank you.*

After reading the note I gazed up to talk to him, but he had vanished. The message was cryptic and sincere—so vampire.

For the following two days the school resumed its undead night life. Students attended classes, teachers taught curriculum, and locals ignored us. Alessandro took Xiu and Joy, the injured vampires, to a hospital in Amsterdam for dental surgery. Their teeth looked good but they would never be able to feed properly through their fangs. Alessandro also assured me that the mess I had left below ground was taken care of.

I sent Gavin a sanitized version of how I caught the Fang Hunter. He replied, "You need to get away from that place, Rebel. It's trouble." I sent him a happy face. No doubt the werewolf would grill me for details at our next family dinner.

The usual rhythm of my life at the academy resumed, almost as if nothing had happened. But Onyx remained missing.

On the third day, he appeared in the doorway of my office with a stern expression. “I have a question,” he said in that low baritone voice that sends shivers up my spine.

“Oh, what’s that?”

“Why are naked mages marching around the academy?”

I ran to the window faster than the speed of light. Sure enough, twenty mages exposing all their male bits walked counterclockwise around the academy.

My heart soared. “Yes!” I said and saluted them.

Harvey hopped out of his chair and did his own version of a bhangra dance. I would have joined him if Onyx wasn’t watching me.

The dhamphyre’s breath heated the back of my neck as I looked outside. “What did you do?” he asked.

“It’s payback, baby, payback. You of all people know that it’s not wise to cross me.” I turned to face him.

His eyes narrowed. “I may regret asking you this, but as head of security I must know. Why are the mages showing us their willies?” His lips tugged on the edges as if he might actually smile. “I need to know the why of it, Rebel.”

I grinned so hard my cheeks hurt. “It’s great, isn’t it?”

“Rebel. What happened?”

“It’s really your fault.”

“Rebel?”

“I went undercover in the mage guild and—”

Shock rippled across his hard face. “You? Undercover?” He chuckled.

“What’s so funny? “

“Honey, everything about you is feminine. Your scent.

Your body." He cleared his throat. "Even the way you walk. No undercover cloak could hide that."

His words warmed me. Onyx relished my femininity! Now, I knew I shouldn't care about that, but ... I did. I really did. The cold-blooded night stalker saw me as a woman!

He blew out a short breath. "What made you do such a stupid thing?"

Stupid? Sheesh. How to end my gushy feelings. Onyx could write a book on that subject. "I was looking for the Fang Hunter."

"And the mages caught you in their guild house."

I nodded.

He tilted his head. "What did they do to you?"

Anyone who knew mages, knew they would never let such a trespass go unpunished. The feelings of that moment of shame, hit me harder than a punch to the gut.

I swallowed and stared at the floor. I would never forget how they humiliated me. Emotion swamped my senses. My hands trembled so hard I fisted them. My cheeks burned.

Onyx waited.

"I ... I had to walk the ... walk of shame."

"I'll kill them."

"No," I shouted to his back as he headed for the door.

He spun to face me. "No one, hurts *you*."

"Onyx, I lived to tell the tale. And look at them now with their drooping dicks exposed for all the world to see. They won't cross me again."

He glanced out the window. He shook his head. The mages raised posters in front of their lower parts that read, Witches rule.

I pulled out my phone to capture the moment.

"It's not wise to cross Rebel you," Onyx commented. A storm of emotions flickered across his face. I imagined he remembered our fights. How could he not. Over the last year both of us risked everything to be rid of each other. It had become a supernatural battle of wills.

"Hmm," he said after a moment. "So, what did you do to bring them here like this? It better be something bloody awful, or else I will kill them, one by one, starting with the Lugnut twit."

I smiled. "My revenge was sweet. I had René put three targeted viruses in their X accounts. You know he's very inventive. And so am I. Our first virus froze the mages' out of their accounts. The second sent out obscene messages on their behalf. And the third, my favorite, tweeted their conspiratorial comments against foreign countries."

Onyx's mouth ticked up on one side. "That's why we have foreign spies roaming through Mystic Keep."

"Probably," I said.

He chuckled. "It's never wise to cross a witch—especially if her name is Rebel." His words tickled my ears.

"Now, you're getting it."

CHARACTERS

Central Characters

•**Rebel** – a half fae/half sorceress, book nerd tasked to run a school for vampire delinquents

•**Onyx** – a night stalker who runs security for the Fangsters academy and slides in and out of the shadows

•**Alessandro** – a drop-dead gorgeous vampire who deals in secrets and makes Rebel's life a nightmare

•**Harvey** – Rebel's mischievous rabbit familiar who happens to be invisible to most others

*Norm - the norm janitor who serves coffee with good stories

<u>Rebel's Local Family</u>

•**Gavin McGee** – Rebel's brother-in-law and Jane's mate, also the werewolf sheriff

•**Donovan O'Reilly** – Rebel's brother-in-law and Merlina's husband, also the sheriff of the supernatural police force in town.

AKNOWLEDGEMENTS

My deepest gratitude goes to:

My Editor, Jacqui Nelson. This was one of the last stories she edited for me before she stopped her editing gig. She now spends all her time writing her own stories and traveling. I feel very lucky to have benefitted from her expertise.

My fantastic proofreader, Tammy Payne, who is a marvel at finding all the typos and blunders. I couldn't publish without you, Tammy. You are the best!

Thanks also go to Winston, my friends, and family who love me on my good and bad writing days, and cheer me on in all my creative projects. I am so grateful for you all.

And finally, I'd like to thank you, the reader, who so generously took the time to read my story. I hope you enjoyed it.

WHAT TO READ NEXT?

The next book in this series, To Fang or Not to Fang, will release next year.

***

Want to read more books by Jo-Ann Carson? Here are the last three Supernatural Suspense series that all took place in Mystic Keep.

Fangster Series

Dial Witch Trilogy

The Perfect Brew Trilogy

Here is a link to my new contemporary cozy mystery series:

Anna Maple Cozy Mysteries

More novels and novellas can be found on my website:

https://Jo-AnnCarson.com

ABOUT THE AUTHOR

Jo-Ann Carson

~ cozy mystery & supernatural suspense~

Jo-Ann Carson writes powerful stories filled with evocative settings, strong characters, and fast-paced plots. Her stories fall into two main genre categories, supernatural suspense and cozy mystery.

Currently she is working on two projects. The open-ended Anna Maple Cozy Mystery series which is about a retired Canadian nurse who keeps finding dead bodies. The second is a five-book urban fantasy series called *Fangsters*, which is the story of a book nerd sorceress blackmailed into running an academy for delinquent, teenage vampires.

To date, Jo-Ann Carson has published 37 stories. Her latest fantasy series include: Fangsters, the Dial Witch Trilogy, The Perfect Brew Trilogy, the Ghost & Abby Mysteries, and the Gambling Ghosts Novellas.

A firm believer in the magic of our everyday lives, Jo-Ann loves watching sunrises, walking the beaches with her poodle near her home in the Pacific Northwest, and reading books by a crackling wood fire. You can find more about her on her website.

Website / Goodreads / BookBub / Facebook / Pinterest

AUTHOR'S NOTE

Thank you for reading my novella. I truly hope you enjoyed reading it as much as I enjoyed writing it. The characters in the Fangsters world are truly a hoot. If you want to learn more about me check out my website, https://www.jo-anncarson.com. If you want to help me as a writer, please write a review for the story on your favorite book site.

Wishing you all the best.

With Gratitude,

Jo-Ann

www.ingramcontent.com/pod-product-compliance
Lightning Source LLC
LaVergne TN
LVHW010115170826
845678LV00012B/2414
* 9 7 8 1 9 8 9 0 3 1 6 4 3 *